Chinese Tale Series

中 国 神 话 故 事

Ne Zha Shaking the Seas

哪 吒 闹 海

Adapted by Chu Yi
Translated by Liu Guangdi
Illustrated by Wang Weizhi

改编　初　旖
翻译　刘光第
绘画　王味之

DOLPHIN BOOKS
海 豚 出 版 社

First Edition 2005

ISBN 978-7-80138-557-4

© Dolphin Books, Beijing, 2005

Published by Dolphin Books

24 Baiwanzhuang Road, Beijing 100037,China

Printed in the People's Republic of China

陳塘

陳塘關

In the last years of the Shang Dynasty, Emperor Zhou was very fatuous and self-indulgent. A great drought happened, lasting for three years, and the Dragon King in the East Sea also often came out to make trouble. So, the common people's life was extremely miserable.

　　商代末年，国君纣王昏庸无道，时值天下三年大旱，加上东海龙王也经常出来兴风作浪，弄得百姓民不聊生。

Li Jing, the general commander at Chentang Pass on the side of the East Sea, was burning with anxiety all day long. Another thing that had been worrying him was his wife did not give birth to a child even after three-year pregnancy.

东海边的陈塘关总兵李靖整日忧心忡忡，看着夫人怀孕三年却还没有生下孩子，更是一筹莫展。

"Your lady has delivered her child! Your lady has delivered her child!" The servant girl ran to tell Li Jing in panic one day.

"夫人生了，夫人生了！"一天，只见丫环惊慌失措地跑来报告李靖。

中国神话故事

Li Jing found his wife had fainted, and to his great surprise, what she delivered was a scarlet flesh ball. Considering the long drought, he concluded that it must be a jinx.

　　李靖发现夫人晕过去了，而生出来的居然是一个鲜红的肉球，联想到天下久旱不雨，认为这一定是个不祥之物。

Li Jing raised his treasured sword to hack the flesh ball.

李靖举起宝剑，就朝肉球劈去。

中国神话故事

When the sharp sword cut into the flesh ball, it suddenly began to whirl, looking transparent and glittering, and sent out golden light, rings upon rings. By now, his wife also woke up.

当剑锋快劈到肉球的时侯，肉球突然开始旋转，通体晶莹透亮，并且放出层层金灿灿的光华。这时总兵夫人也醒来了。

Everyone present was gazing at the strange flesh ball in astonishment. It changed slowly, and in a while, it turned into a lotus in bud. The petals opened slowly, and on the seedpod of the middle of the lotus was sleeping a lovely male baby.

大家惊讶地看着这个奇异的肉球，肉球正在慢慢变化，一会儿功夫，竟化做一朵含苞待放的荷花。花瓣慢慢开放，在花心的莲蓬上，正睡着一个可爱的男娃娃。

哪吒闹海

The baby grew very fast, and in a short while, it stood up, opened his eyes, yawned, stretched his little arms, looked at Li Jing and his wife, and cried clearly, "Papa,Papa,Mom,Mom." The family began to cheer happily at the scene.

娃娃长得很快，不一会儿就站起来，睁开了眼睛，打了一个呵欠，伸了伸小胳膊，望着李靖和夫人清脆地叫着："爸爸，爸爸，妈妈，妈妈！"见此情景，一家人乐坏了。

At this moment, a white-bearded old man riding a crane descended from the sky, and it turned out to be God Taiyi, an immortal from Heaven, "General Li and Your Lady, I congratulate you on getting a dear son. This child is a lucky fruit of heaven and earth, and he will bring peace to the world. Please let him be my pupil!" Li Jing and his wife were very glad.

这时一个白胡子老头儿乘鹤而降，原来是天上的神仙太乙真人来了。

"恭喜李总兵和夫人喜得贵子，这个孩子是天地的造化，他将会给天下带来太平。就让他做我的徒儿吧！"李靖夫妇高兴极了。

Taiyi gave the baby a name, "Nezha", and offered him two treasures, one was a gold ring called "Qiankun Ring" (in Chinese, "qiankun" means the universe), and the other a long piece of damask silk called "Huntian Silk" ("huntian" means "heaven" in Chinese). They were said to be god-given treasures in the universe, and would protect Nezha. After making clear all the matter, God Taiyi flew away riding his crane.

太乙给娃娃起了个名字叫哪吒，并送给他两件宝物：一个金圈叫乾坤圈，一条长绫叫混天绫，是天地间难得的宝物，它们会保护哪吒。交代完毕，太乙真人就乘鹤飞走了。

哪吒闹海

中国神话故事

Nezha was rejoiced. One day, Nezha and his little fellow were playing at the sea front. Suddenly, boiling waves came up in the sea, and on the crest were standing the yaksha and his shrimp soldiers and crab generals. Without saying anything, they lifted a wave to swallow Nezha's little friend into the sea. It turned out that they came to catch a child to offer to the Dragon King as his refection.

哪吒有了两件宝物可开心了。一天，哪吒和小伙伴正在海边玩耍。突然海上起了大浪，浪头上站着夜叉精和虾兵蟹将。他们不由分说，掀起一个浪头就把哪吒的小伙伴卷到海里去了。原来他们是来捉小孩儿献给龙王当点心吃的。

By one flip, Nezha jumped onto the stone reef, and pointing to the yaksha, he asked him to return his friend. The yaksha had a good laugh, and raised his steel fork, wanting to take Nezha away together.

Nezha became furious, he threw out his Qiankun Ring, just hitting the forehead of the yaksha, and the yaksha was battered to death at once. The shrimp soldiers and crab generals turned pale with fright, and hurried into the sea to take the message to their superiors.

　　哪吒一个筋斗跳到石礁上，指着夜叉要他还回伙伴，夜叉哈哈大笑，举起钢叉就要连哪吒一起捉去。

　　哪吒大怒，挥出乾坤圈，正砸在夜叉的脑门上，只一下就把夜叉砸死了。虾兵蟹将大惊失色，慌忙钻到海里报信去了。

哪吒闹海

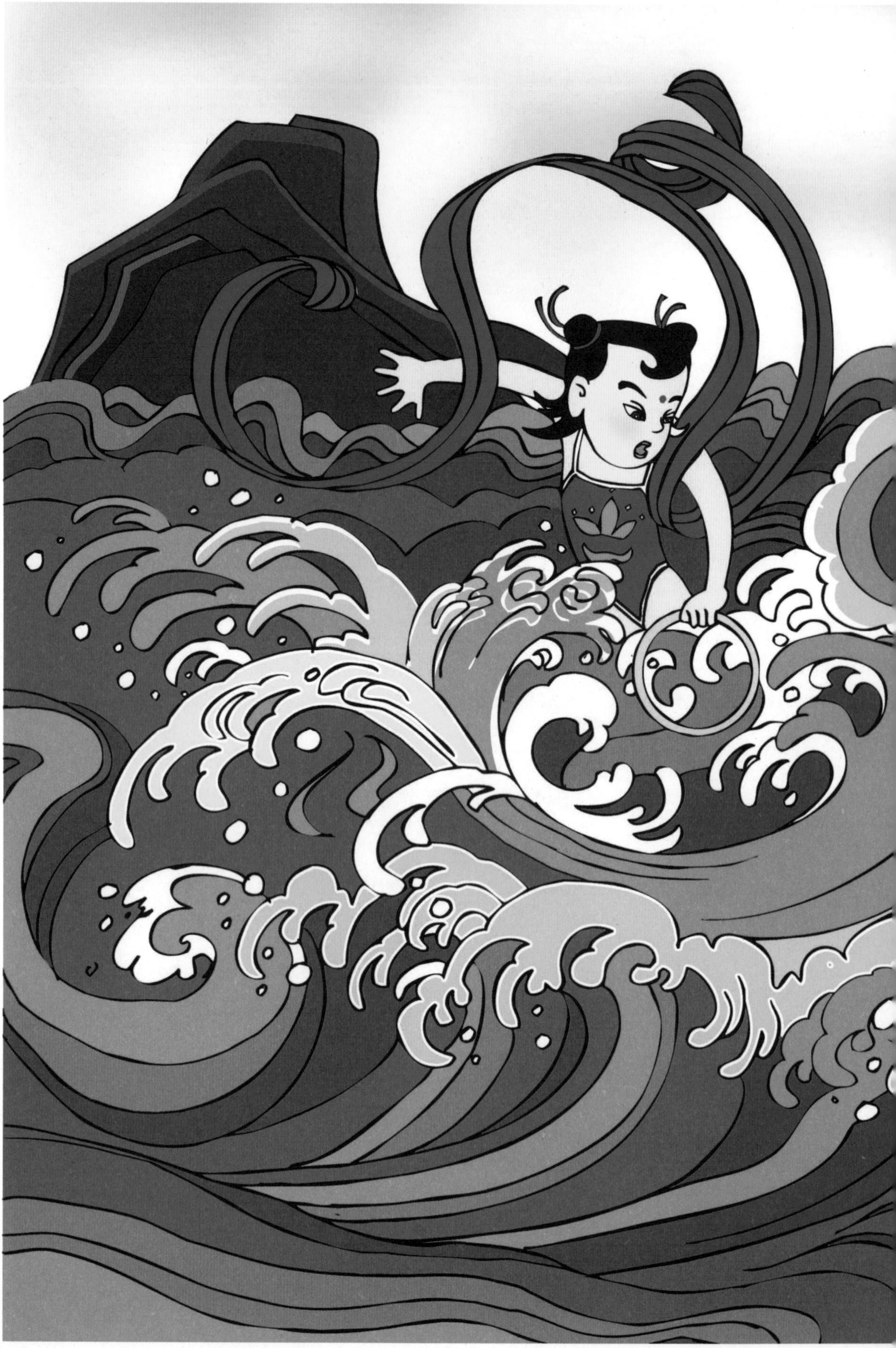

"Damned monster, it has dirtied my Qiankun Ring!" Nezha began to wash his Qiankun Ring in the seawater.But his washing stirred a great popple of the sea. Nezha was very excited, and shouted to the sea,"Return my friend, be quick, return my friend." While shouting, Nezha swayed the ring, so the whole sea became turbulent.

"死海怪，把我的乾坤圈弄脏了！"哪吒在海水里洗起他的乾坤圈来。这一洗不要紧，搅得大海翻滚起来。哪吒一看非常兴奋，朝着海里大声喊道："快把我的伙伴送回来，快把我的伙伴送回来。"哪吒边说边晃，整个大海动荡得更历害了。

17

哪吒闹海

The Dragon King of the East Sea was greatly shocked,"Ah? Who is stirring the sea?" The shrimp soldiers and crab generals told the Dragon King that the yaksha had been beaten to death by a child. "Father, let me find out who is so rude, and I will catch him here." The third prince of the Dragon King was asking for a battle assignment.

东海龙王大惊失色:"啊?是什么人敢搅动大海!"虾兵蟹将把夜叉被一个小孩儿打死的事报告了龙王。"父王,让孩儿去看看是什么人敢如此放肆,待孩儿把他擒来。"龙三太子主动请战。

The third prince was a presumptuous guy, just like
the old Dragon King, he never abided by the rules,
and thought nothing of anyone else.

龙三太子是一个狂妄的家伙，他和老龙王一
样，从来不讲道理，并且从不把任何人放在眼里。

When Nezha was just in high spirits, a higher wave came suddenly, and the third prince appeared with his shrimp soldiers and crab generals. "It is just that kid." The shrimp soldiers and crab generals shouted, pointing to Nezha.

Nezha shouted to them, "Monsters, why have you not taken my friend back to me?" Without listening to any words of Nezha, the third prince began to strike him with the fork.

哪吒正晃得来劲呢，突然海上冲起一个更高的浪头，上面出现了龙三太子和众虾兵蟹将。"就是那个小孩儿。"虾兵蟹将指着哪吒叫嚷着。

哪吒一看又来人了，喊到："妖怪，为什么还没把我的伙伴送回来？"龙三太子根本不听哪吒说话，举叉就打。

哪吒闹海

The third prince had reckoned that he could strike Nezha to death by one blow, but to his surprise, when the fork struck Nezha's Qiankun Ring, he got such a great shock that his arms became numb. He was furious and cried madly. A fierce fight began.

　　龙三太子本想一下就可以把哪吒打死，可没想到叉碰到了哪吒的乾坤圈，震得他两臂发麻。他被气得哇哇怪叫，一场大战开始了。

中
国
神
话
故
事

哪吒闹海

Just after a few rounds, the third prince found he was no match for Nezha, so he changed himself into a silver dragon, wanting to escape into the sea, but he was tied by Nezha's Huntian Silk.

不过几个回合，龙三太子眼见战不过哪吒，慌忙化做一条银龙要往海里钻，却被哪吒的混天绫捆住了。

The dragon prince was dragged by Nezha to the beach. He had never been treated like this, he was so angry that his muscles bulged.

"Why do you catch small children?" Treading on the prince, Nezha questioned him.

"Hum, that is the top-grade refection of our dragon family. We have eaten uncountable children!" The prince said in a distaining tone.

Nezha was furious at the words, so he swung his Qiankun Ring and beat the prince to death just by one blow. Then he took out the sinew from the dragon.

龙三太子被哪吒拖到海滩上，他哪里有过这样的遭遇，气得龙筋都鼓起来了。

"你们为什么要捉小孩儿？"哪吒踩着龙三太子大声质问。

"哼，那是我们龙家族的上品点心，我们不知吃了多少小孩儿了呢！"龙三太子不屑地说。

哪吒气坏了，抢起乾坤圈，一下就把龙三太子打死了，还把龙筋也抽了出来。

哪吒闹海

The shrimp soldiers and crab generals dared not make any attack at all. Nezha threw the prince's corpse into the sea.

虾兵蟹将不敢向前。哪吒把龙三太子的尸体扔到了海里。

哪
吒
闹
海

"Tell the old Dragon King, if they go on eating children, I will beat all of them to death!" Nezha shouted to the shrimp soldiers and crab generals. The shrimp soldiers and crab generals were frightened. In a flurry, they carried the dead body of the third prince and ran back into the sea.

　　"告诉老龙王，他们要是再敢吃小孩儿，我就把他们全都打死！"哪吒朝虾兵蟹将们喊道。吓得虾兵蟹将们驮起龙三太子的尸体，慌慌张张地钻到海里去了。

"Papa,Papa,I have killed the third dragon prince. They will never catch children again. I give this dragon sinew to you, and you may make a girdle with it!" Little Nezha handed the dragon sinew to his father excitedly.

　　"爸爸,爸爸,我把龙三太子打死了,它们再也不敢捉小孩儿了,这根龙筋给您做条腰带吧!"小哪吒兴奋地把龙筋递给爸爸。

Li Jing was so shocked by the act of his 7-year-old son that he could not speak for a time. After a long while, he said, covering his head with his hands, "Nezha, you have brought a great disaster!"

　　李靖被自己这个 7 岁小儿子的举动惊得说不出话来，半晌，他捂着自己的头说："哪吒呀，你闯下大祸了！"

29

哪吒闹海

Suddenly, it became dark all round, and they could hear roaring thunder and see dazzling lightning. All the Dragon Kings of the four seas appeared in the clouds. After hearing his son was killed by Nezha, the Dragon King of the East Sea knew he was no match for Nezha, so he called the Dragon Kings of the other three seas to deal with Nezha.

忽然间天昏地暗，电闪雷鸣。云层里现出四海龙王。原来东海龙王看到自己的儿子被哪吒打死了，知道自己不是哪吒的对手，立刻就把其他的海龙王招来一起对付哪吒。

"Li Jing, surrender Nezha to me immediately! I will take revenge for my son." The old Dragon King of the East Sea was bellowing to Li Jing.

"Your Majesty, my son is only 7 years old, and still ignorant of the rules. Please forgive us!" Li Jing pleaded for his son.

"Elder brother, don't listen to him, just make it hot for them!" All the Dragon Kings of the four seas exercised their power together,a downpour came down to Chentang Pass directly.

"李靖,快把哪吒交出来,我要为我的儿子报仇。"东海老龙王对着李靖怒吼着。

"龙王,我的小儿才7岁,尚不懂事,请龙王原谅!"李靖赶忙为哪吒求情。

"大哥,不要听他啰嗦,先给他们点儿颜色看看!"南海、北海、西海龙王和东海龙王一起发威,倾盆大雨直接倾泻到陈塘关。

The water level rose at once, the people's houses began to collapse, so people fled out of their houses one after another. Chentang Pass was to be submerged by the flood soon. The Dragon Kings of the four seas shuttled back and forth in the clouds, continuing to make the downpour madly.

The common people fleeing for life, Nezha got very anxious, and shouted angrily to the Dragon Kings,"Dragon Kings, it is I who killed the prince, and it has nothing to do with the common people of Chentang Pass. Don't harm them, you may do anything you like to me only!"

"OK, I want you to pay your life for my son!" The Dragon King of the East Sea roared ferociously.

水位很快上涨，百姓的房子开始倒塌，人们纷纷逃出屋子，陈塘关眼看就要被大水淹没了。四海龙王穿梭在云层中，继续疯狂地喷着大雨。

哪吒焦急地看着逃命的百姓，愤怒地对着龙王高声喊道："龙王，打死龙三太子的人是我，与陈塘关的百姓无关，你放过他们，我任凭你发落！"

"好，我要你为我儿子偿命！"东海龙王恶狠狠地吼道。

"You should keep your word."

"I guarantee, with my status as the Dragon King of the East Sea." Dragon King yelped while gnashing his teeth.

Looking at the fleeing people, with tears running down his face, Nezha took out his father's sword, and killed himself at once. Since Nezha had already died, the Dragon King of the East Sea dropped away with all the other sea gods.

"你说话算话?"

"我以东海龙王的身份担保。"龙王咬牙切齿地叫着。

望着奔逃的百姓们，哪吒含着泪，抽出了父亲的宝剑，自刎而死。东海龙王看到哪吒死了，也带着众海神散去了。

中国神话故事

At this moment, a red-crowned crane flew up, and
took away the rising soul of Nezha with its beak.
Seeing Nezha's soul, God Taiyi smiled,"You are
really a promising child, I will save you."

　　这时一只丹顶鹤从空中飞来，含走了哪吒正
在升起的魂魄。
　　太乙真人看着哪吒的魂魄，微笑着说："你是
个有出息的好孩子，我会救活你的。"

哪吒闹海

中国神话故事

God Taiyi used lotus flowers, some lotus leafs and a lotus root to make a human shape, he put Nezha's soul into the lotus, and then blew a puff of air lightly to it. Thus, a new Nezha was born from the lotus.

太乙真人用荷花、荷叶和莲藕摆出了一个人的形状，把哪吒的魂魄放在荷花上，轻轻地在上面吹了口气，一个莲花化身的哪吒诞生了。

"Master!" Hugging his master, Nezha was in a flood of tears.

"师父！"哪吒搂着师父，泪如雨下。

"Nezha, you will bring justice and peace to the turbid world." God Taiyi offered Nezha a pair of Wind-Fire Wheels, and taught him the theurgy to change himself into a being with three heads and six arms. The newborn Nezha was more powerful now.

"哪吒，你会给混乱的天下带来正义和太平的。"太乙真人又送给哪吒一对风火轮，传给了哪吒变化三头六臂的法术。新生的哪吒本领更大了。

哪
吒
闹
海

中国神话故事

While a celebration dinner was going on in the dragon palace because of the death of Nezha, the shrimp general came to report,"Your Majesty, a bad thing has happened, Nezha has broken into our palace!" The Dragon Kings were astounded, and before they came to, Nezha had already shown up before them.

The four Dragon Kings had to lead their troops to meet him.

龙宫里正在为除掉哪吒开庆功宴呢，虾将来报："大王，出祸事了，哪吒打到龙宫来了！"龙王们大吃一惊，还没回过神来，哪吒已出现在他们面前。

四海龙王慌忙率兵迎战。

Of course, they were no match for Nezha. Finally, the Dragon Kings admitted defeat, begging for mercy again and again.

他们哪里是哪吒的对手。最后龙王们终于服输了，连连求饶。

"I can forgive you, but you must promise two things for me."
"All right, all right, even ten things! Say them quickly, little hero."
"First, make a good rain for all the common people in the world, and be sure to let the world have favorable climate all the time; Second, never harm children."

A timely rain fell in the world, and all the plants regained their vitality. The Dragon Kings never came out to make trouble again. Later, Nezha helped the wise powerful ruler, Emperor Wu of the Zhou Dynasty, to overthrow the tyrant king, Emperor Zhou of the Shang Dynasty, and established the Zhou Dynasty. The world became peaceful at last. From then on, Nezha became the most famous little hero in China.

"我可以饶了你们，但你们必须依我两件事。"

"依的，依的，十件也依的，小英雄快说。"

"第一，速给天下百姓普降甘雨，必须让天下风调雨顺；第二，不得再害小孩子了。"

天下普降了一场甘霖，花草树木庄稼又恢复了生机，海龙王再也不敢出来作乱了。后来，哪吒辅佐明君周武王，灭掉了昏君商纣王，建立了周朝，使天下得以太平。从此，哪吒成为中国最有名的小英雄。

图书在版编目 （CIP）数据

哪吒闹海 / 初旖改编；王味之绘；刘光第译.
北京：海豚出版社，2005.10
（中国神话故事）
ISBN 978-7-80138-557-4

I. 哪... II. ①初... ②王... ③刘... III. 图画故
事—中国—当代—英汉 IV. I287.8

中国版本图书馆 CIP 数据核字（2005）第 115080 号

中国神话故事

哪吒闹海

改编：初　旖
绘画：王味之
翻译：刘光第
社址：北京百万庄大街 24 号　　　邮编：100037
印刷：北京地大彩印厂
开本：16 开（787 毫米 × 1092 毫米）
文种：英汉　　印张：3
版次：2005 年 10 月第 1 版 2009 年 4 月第 4 次印刷
标准书号：ISBN 978-7-80138-557-4
定价：15.00 元